Mary Had a Little Lamb

WRITTEN BY
SARAH JOSEPHA HALE

PHOTO-ILLUSTRATED AND AFTERWORD BY
BRUCE McMILLAN

SCHOLASTIC INC. ○ NEW YORK

Design and drawings by Bruce McMillan
Art direction by Claire Counihan
Text set in Scotch 2
Color separations by Color Dot
Original edition printed by Rae
Original edition bound by Horowitz

Library of Congress Cataloging-in-Publication Data

Hale, Sarah Josepha Buell, 1788-1879.
Mary had a little lamb.

Summary: A contemporary interpretation of the well-known
nineteenth-century nursery rhyme about the school-going lamb.
Accompanied by color photographs, a sample exercise from
McGuffey's reader, and a note on the history of the author
and her famous rhyme.
1. Lambs—Juvenile poetry. 2. Children's poetry,
American. [1. Nursery rhymes. 2. American poetry]
I. McMillan, Bruce, ill. II. Title.
PS1774.H2M3 1990   811'.2   89-24391
ISBN 0-590-43773-9

12 11 10 9 8 7 6 5 4 3 2   1 2 3 4 5/9

Printed in the U.S.A.   36

First Scholastic printing, September 1990

For Miss Parker,
the dedicated
teacher

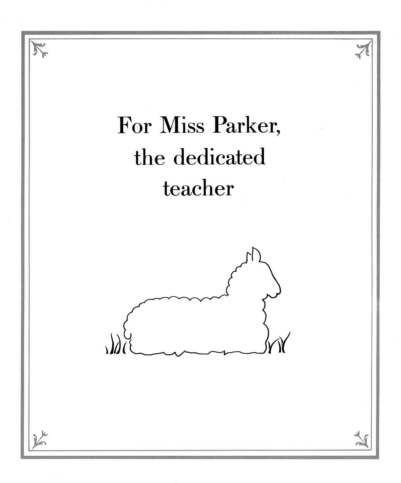

Mary had a little lamb,

Its fleece was white as snow.

And everywhere that Mary went

The lamb was sure to go.

It followed her to school one day.

That was against the rule.

It made the children laugh and play

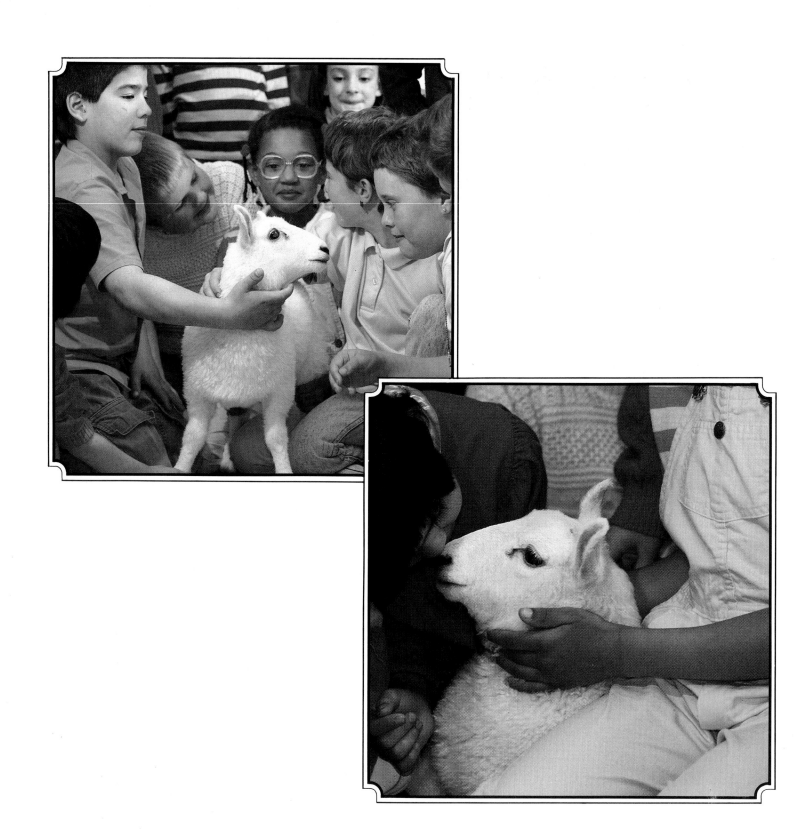

To see a lamb at school.

And so,

The teacher turned it out,

But still it lingered near;

And waited patiently about,

Till Mary did appear.

"Why does the lamb love Mary so?"

The eager children cry.

"Why, Mary loves the lamb you know,"

The teacher did reply.

AFTERWORD

The poem, *Mary Had a Little Lamb*, was first published in 1830 under the title *Mary's Lamb*. It was an immediate success. It was printed on silk handkerchiefs and sold in Boston bookstores. Currier & Ives made a print of Mary and her lamb. In 1834 the words were set to music and published by Mrs. Hale in her *School Song Book*. In 1844 the poem was published as a lesson in *The First Eclectic Reader*, the most popular schoolbook of its day. William McGuffey, the schoolbook's writer and editor, did not credit Mrs. Hale, and the poem became known as a Mother Goose rhyme.

In 1877, the verse was immortalized when Thomas Edison made a phonograph recording. "Mary had a little lamb" became the first words of recorded human speech.

The verse has endured but has undergone changes beyond its title since it was first published in 1830. The familiar contemporary verse appears in this book. Compared to the original, the contemporary version has undergone two significant changes. The poem known today has been shortened by eight lines. Also, the poem known today refers to the lamb as "it." The original reference was to a male lamb. For comparison, this is the original form as it appeared in the 1830 edition of *Poems for Our Children*, by Mrs. Sarah Josepha Hale, published by Marsh, Capen & Lyon.

MARY'S LAMB
(original version)

Mary had a little lamb,
  Its fleece was white as snow,
And everywhere that Mary went
  The lamb was sure to go;
He* followed her to school one day —
  That was against the rule,
It made the children laugh and play,
  To see a lamb at school.

And so the Teacher turned him* out,
  But still he* lingered near,
And waited patiently about,
  Till Mary did appear;
And then he* ran to her, and laid **
  His* head upon her arm, **
As if he* said — 'I'm not afraid — **
  You'll keep me from all harm.' **

'What makes the lamb love Mary so?'
  The eager children cry —
'O, Mary loves the lamb, you know,'
  The Teacher did reply;
'And you each gentle animal **
  In confidence may bind,**
And make them follow at your call, **
  If you are always *kind*.' **

* reference to lamb as a male
** original line, not in contemporary poem

McGUFFEY'S OLD SECOND READER
1857

Lesson XLVII

lamb	ap-pear'	re-ply'	a-gainst'
fleece	ea'ger	fol'low	chil'dren
laugh	Ma'ry	wait'ed	an'i-mal
school	lin'ger-*ed*	teach'er	pa'tient-ly

Exercises

What did Mary have?

Where did the lamb go with Mary?

What did the lamb do?

Why did he love Mary?

ABOUT THIS BOOK

Mary Had a Little Lamb was written by a Sarah and features another Sarah. The Mary in this book is Sarah Jackson, a first-grade student from Kennebunk, Maine. If Sarah looks like a charming and caring youngster in this story, it's because she truly is one.

The lamb's name is Argyle. He is a registered Border Cheviot and lives on Ron "The Shepherd" Prévoir's farm.

The book was photographed at Mr. Prévoir's Shapleigh Knoll Farm in Shapleigh, Maine, and at the Alfred (Maine) Elementary School. The Alfred school was selected because of the architectural use of the original Alfred school bell. The traditional bell and bell tower, set in the design of a modern school, reflect the intent of this book — the interpretation of a traditional verse in a contemporary manner.

The Alfred and Kennebunk students who appear are: Laura Ayotte, Luke Brochu, George Dalglish, John Folsom, III, Royal Haskell, Asa Holt, Emily Lachance, Elizabeth Leddy, Ruth Leddy, Sage Okamoto, Ellen Palminteri, Daniel Perry, and Anna Picard. The teacher in the story, John Seaver, teaches at the Alfred Elementary School.

Research for this book was done at the Richards Free Library, which is in Sarah Josepha Hale's hometown of Newport, New Hampshire.

TECHNICAL DATA

Color was important. Because "its fleece was white as snow," Argyle was gently bathed in the farm's kitchen sink before each photo session. The selection of Mary's vividly colorful yellow-and-pink outfit was intended to draw visual attention to her. Once her outfit was chosen, the rest of the book's colors were coordinated.

Sarah wears eyeglasses. Though many children wear eyeglasses, few photo-illustrated books feature children wearing them. Eyeglasses are usually taken off as the simplest solution to a photographic problem — reflections. I felt it important to see a child wearing glasses. So, reflections were controlled through the use of lighting and a polarizing filter.

This book was photographically sketched and shot using a Nikon FE-2 camera with 50mm, 105mm, and 200mm Nikkor lenses. Outdoor lighting was natural sunlight. A fill reflector was used when possible. A polarizing filter was used to enhance the outdoor color without shifting color balance, and to reduce reflections. Indoor lighting was a combination of a quartz light to warm the color, and multiple off-the-camera electronic flash units to simulate natural daylight color. The film used was Kodachrome 64, processed by Kodalux.